TOOL. TIME. TWIST.

A BRIEF HISTORY OF TOOLS THROUGH TIME

DAVID SHAPIRO   CHRISTOPHER HERNDON

Printed in the United States

ISBN: 9780984442270

Art Director: Erica Melville
Designer: Brian David Smith
Cover Illustrations: Christopher Herndon

CRAIGMORE
CREATIONS

2900 SE Stark St, Suite 1A
Portland, OR 97214

www.craigmorecreations.com

To Louis and all of tomorrow's builders.
-David

WHAT'S THE TOOL?
Sticks and stones!

WHAT'S THE TIME?
2.5 million years ago!

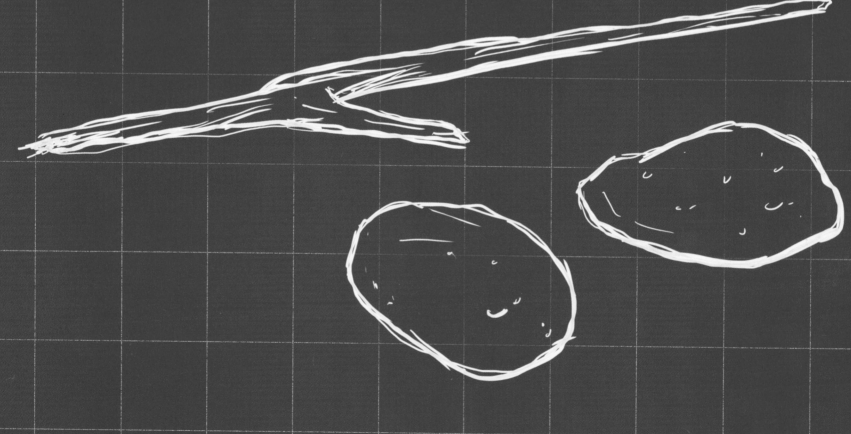

WHAT'S THE TWIST?

Humans and our ancestors are not the only ones to use tools. Otters, octopuses, chimpanzees, and crows have all been known to use them too!

WHAT'S THE TOOL?
The hand ax!

WHAT'S THE TIME?
More than 1.5 million years ago!

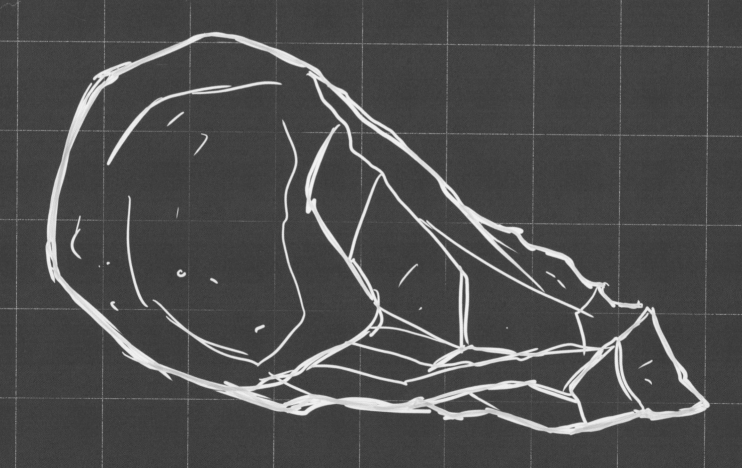

WHAT'S THE TWIST?

The ancestors of humans invented this tool.
Simple as it was, the hand ax helped our
ancestors live in and explore the world from Africa
to Southeast Asia.

WHAT'S THE TOOL?
Fire!

WHAT'S THE TIME?
600,000 years ago
(maybe even 1.5 million years ago)!

WHAT'S THE TWIST?

Great care needs to be taken with this tool! Used properly, fire can cook food, shed light, and keep us warm.

WHAT'S THE TOOL?
Pigments!

WHAT'S THE TIME?
400,000 years ago!

WHAT'S THE TWIST?

Long, long ago, humans began to paint. Using a mix of clay, water, and ground-up rocks, they painted their bodies, their shelters, and the walls of caves.

WHAT'S THE TOOL?
The projectile point!

WHAT'S THE TIME?
100,000 years ago!

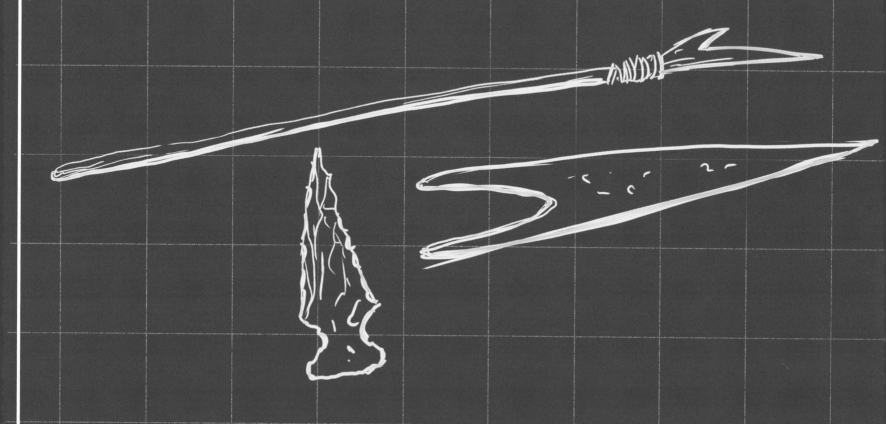

WHAT'S THE TWIST?

The use of spears, darts, and arrows enabled early humans to hunt many more kinds of animals than they ever could before.

WHAT'S THE TOOL?

Glue!

WHAT'S THE TIME?

70,000 years ago!

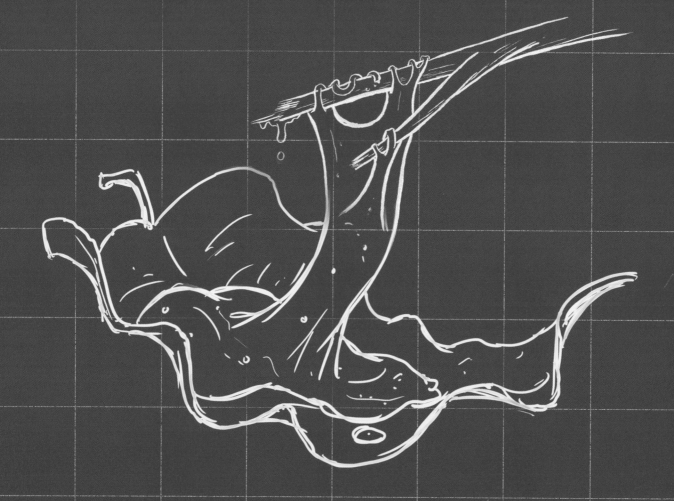

WHAT'S THE TWIST?

Early glue was made from heating and mixing plant gums and tree saps. It was not an easy task, but a hunter's life depended upon a well-glued tool!

WHAT'S THE TOOL?
The calendar!

WHAT'S THE TIME?
35,000 years ago!

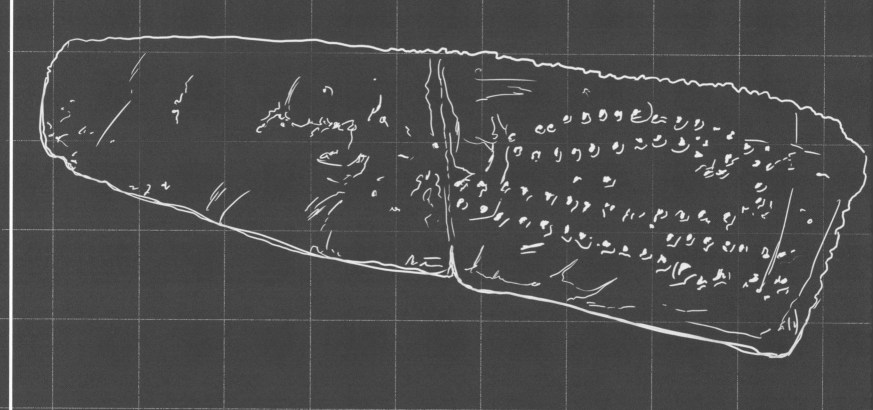

WHAT'S THE TWIST?

Being able to count the days helped our human ancestors keep track of when certain plants and animals would return. Today we still use a calendar to help us plan work, play, and school.

WHAT'S THE TOOL?

The sewing needle!

WHAT'S THE TIME?

30,000 years ago!

WHAT'S THE TWIST?

The use of a needle and thread allowed humans to make clothes to keep warm and protected from the winter winds and made it possible to explore new lands!

WHAT'S THE TOOL?
The bronze ax!

WHAT'S THE TIME?
6,000 years ago!

WHAT'S THE TWIST?

Melting metals together made for a stronger ax that could chop more things! This tool changed the way humans worked with wood, built houses, and made boats.

WHAT'S THE TOOL?

The plow!

WHAT'S THE TIME?

2,100 years ago!

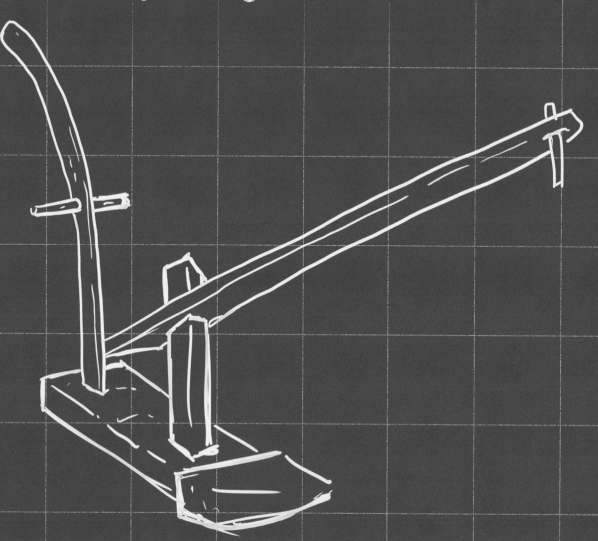

WHAT'S THE TWIST?

This tool sure made farming easier! With the help of a plow, food could be planted faster, leaving more time for family and storytelling.

WHAT'S THE TOOL?
The saw!

WHAT'S THE TIME?
About 2,000 years ago!

24

WHAT'S THE TWIST?

The creation of the saw meant we could make nice straight cuts in wood. The toothed saw was invented in Egypt and was an important part of the pyramid builder's toolbox.

WHAT'S THE TOOL?
The claw hammer!

WHAT'S THE TIME?
1,000 years ago!

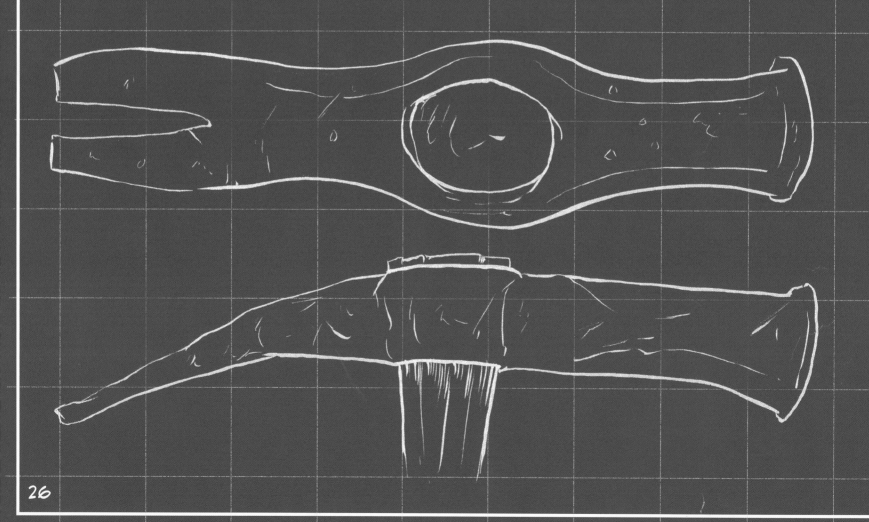

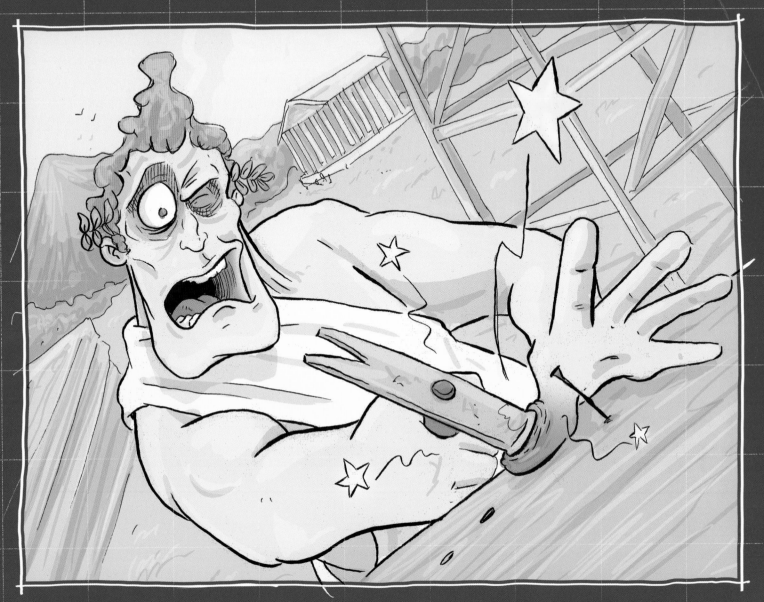

WHAT'S THE TWIST?

Claw hammers first appeared in ancient Rome. They allowed a person to knock a nail in and pull it back out again!

WHAT'S THE TOOL?

The hand brace drill!

WHAT'S THE TIME?

500 years ago!

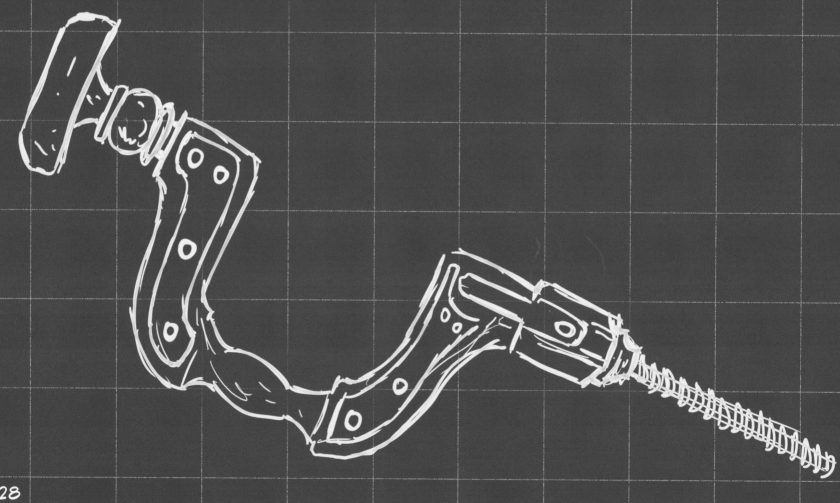

WHAT'S THE TWIST?

The first true drills are thousands of years old, but in medieval times a great improvement was made in the way they worked. The hand brace drill could move around and around and not stop until the hole was made!

WHAT'S THE TOOL?
The wrench!

WHAT'S THE TIME?
1835!

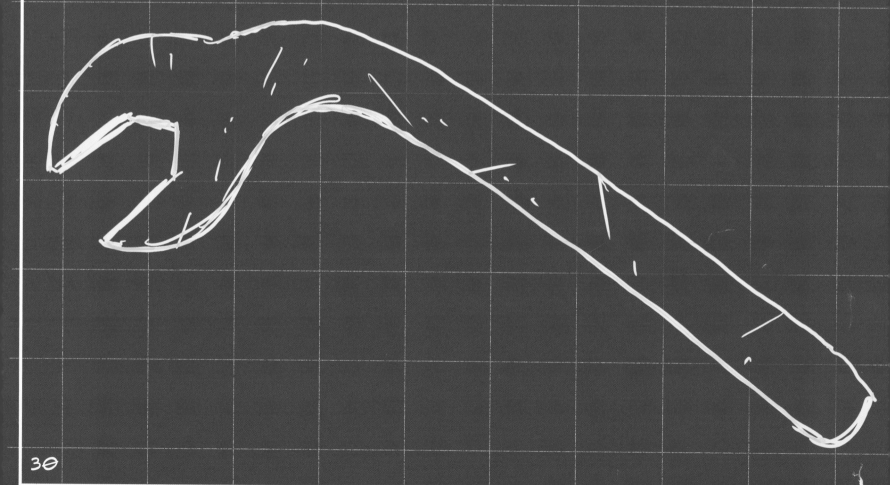

WHAT'S THE TWIST?

The first wrench was made in the United States by a man named Solymon Merrick. Useful for fixing everything from a sink to a bike, this tool is now found in almost every home in the country!

WHAT'S THE TOOL?
The tape measure!

WHAT'S THE TIME?
1868!

WHAT'S THE TWIST?

Tape measures allow us to uniformly measure things both big and small! This important tool was also invented in the United States and is now used by builders all over the world.

WHAT'S THE TOOL?
Portable power tools!

WHAT'S THE TIME?
1895!

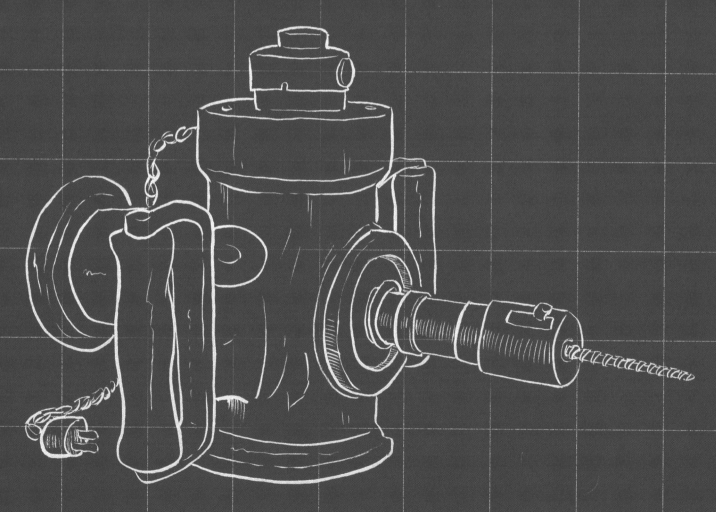

WHAT'S THE TWIST?

Shortly after the invention of the light bulb, a German man named Wilhelm Fein invented the first portable electric drill. Now tough drilling jobs could be done quicker and in more places.

WHAT'S THE TOOL?

The vise grip!

WHAT'S THE TIME?

1924!

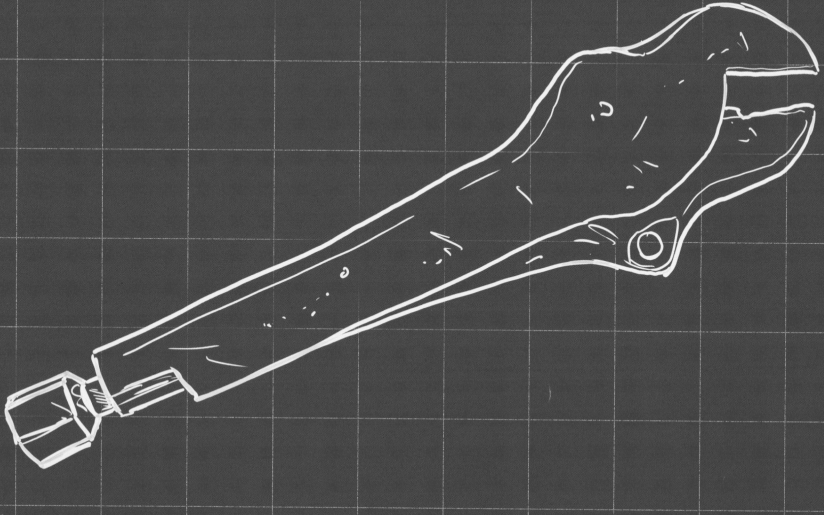

WHAT'S THE TWIST?

Clamp and twist is how a vise grip works. A firm, locked-in grip makes it easier to tighten loose nuts and bolts!

WHAT'S THE TOOL?

Phillips-head screwdriver and screws!

WHAT'S THE TIME?

1930!

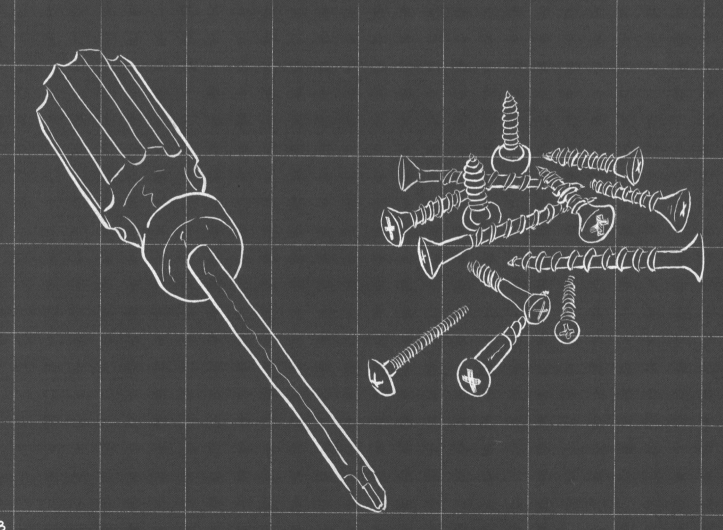

WHAT'S THE TWIST?

These screws can be turned quite tight! When they were invented, they were very important for making cars and airplanes. Now you can find them in many of your toys.

WHAT'S THE TOOL?
The multi-tool!

WHAT'S THE TIME?
1983!

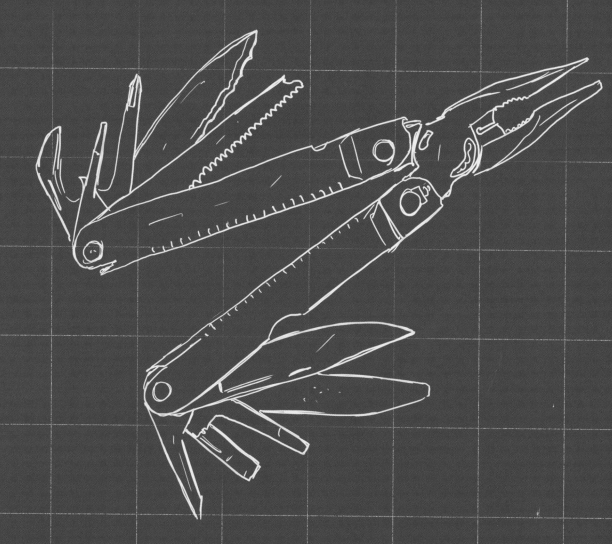

WHAT'S THE TWIST?

It's like having a mini toolbox on your belt! Today, handy men and women use multi-tools for everything from fence building to opening a can of tomato soup.

WHAT'S THE TOOL?

A toolbox!

WHAT'S THE TIME?

All time!

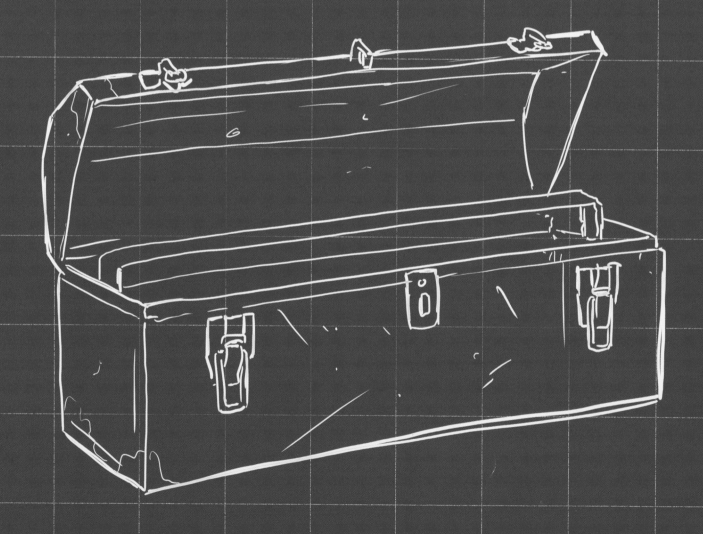

WHAT'S THE TWIST?

There's nothing better than having all your tools organized! A good toolbox helps you keep together everything that you'll need for projects around the home and beyond.

SO THERE YOU HAVE IT:

A brief trip through tool time!

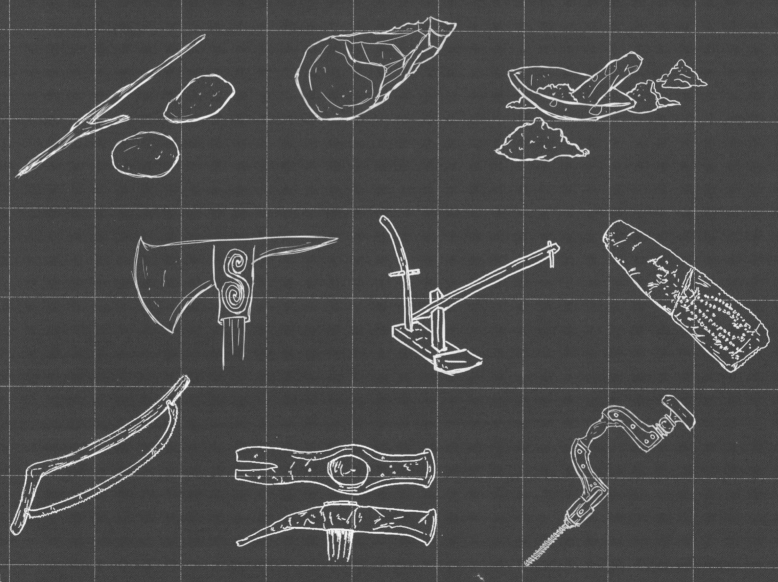

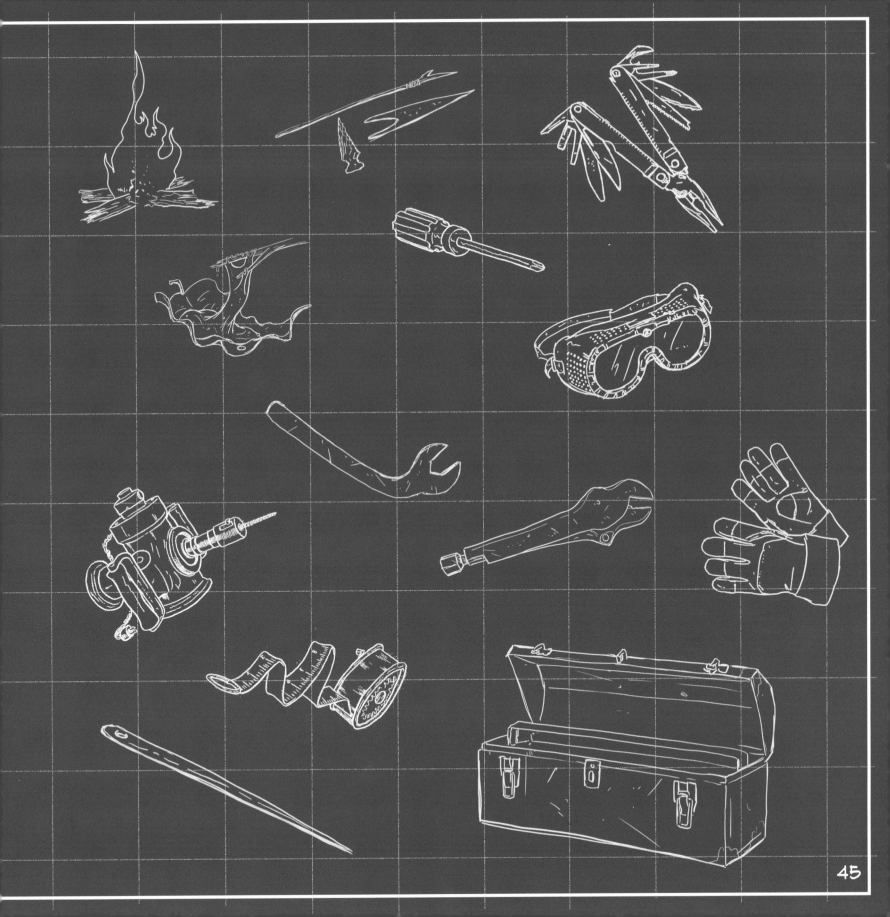

WHAT'S THE TWIST?

From the deep sea to outer space, from the backyard to the playground, tools allow us to build, take apart, and rebuild the objects we love to live, work, and play with!

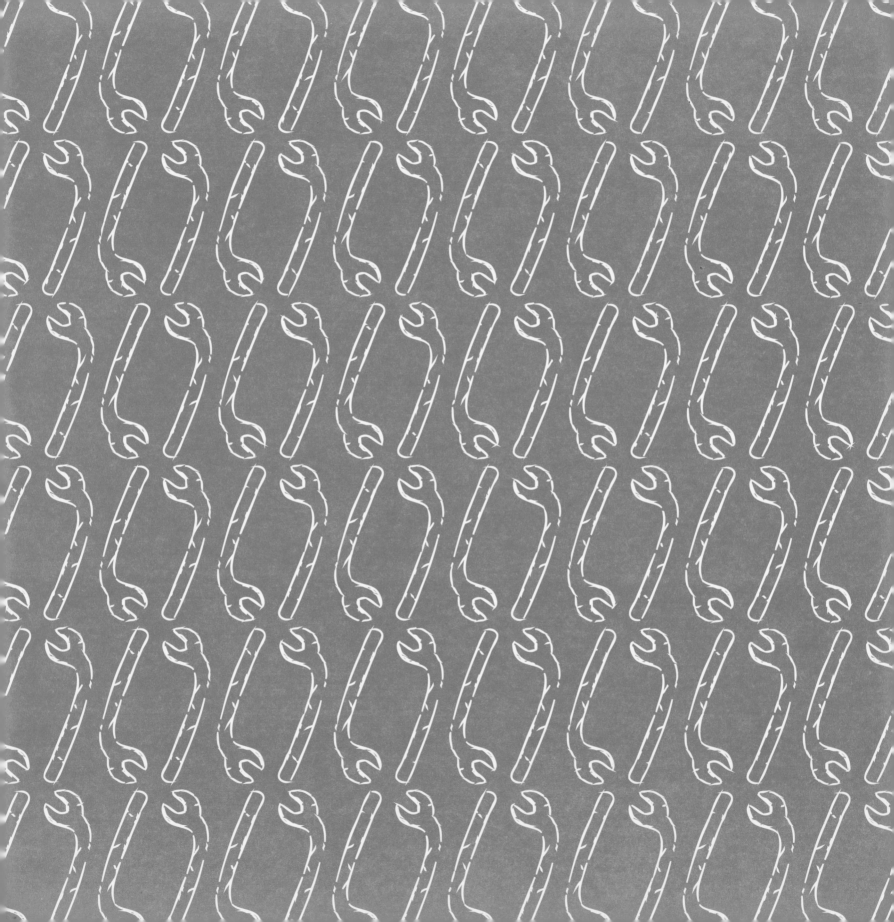